Hi I'm Feely and this is my diary.

There are six Feely books so far. It's best to read them in this order:

Feely's Magic Diary
by Barbara Catchpole
Illustrated by Jan Dolby

Published by Ransom Publishing Ltd.
Unit 7, Brocklands Farm, West Meon, Hampshire GU32 1JN, UK
www.ransom.co.uk

ISBN   978 1785911217
First published in 2016

Feely's Magic Diary

Barbara Catchpole

Illustrated by Jan Dolby

Ransom

Hey you!

I am so happy you are reading my diary! Did you buy it on ebay? Like people buy Posh Spice's old clothes?

Do you think a lot of people have bought it? (My diary, not Posh Spice's old clothes.)

Perhaps – *perhaps* – you're reading this

and I'm already famous! Perhaps I'm lying
on a beach in my fabulous bikini with
diamonds on it, waiting to start my next big
film! R U jealous or what?

Oliver (my useless big brother) is
probably standing next to my sunbed with
the ice to put in my drink. (I wish it wasn't
him though)

Wow! Hang on – I don't have to be dead
for you to buy my diary, do I? Like that

Samuel Peeps guy from history. People shouldn't read diaries of living people – that's private.

Am I dead? Not so happy now (sad face). Not really worth writing a diary if you're dead. (OK, I know – you can't write a diary if you're dead. You can't hold the pen and stuff.)

I'm getting well confused. It's probably because I don't really get time travel. Oliver says it's because I've got a brain the size of a pea He says not even a big pea, but one of those tiny little ones you get from France. They have a name. No, not 'peas'.

Oliver says that's what happened to the dinosaurs. They had tiny brains and they froze to death.

Was it because they were too dumb to knit woolly jumpers? Or they couldn't light fires? Or invent central heating?

8

They ate loads of people in Jurassic

Park though, didn't they, Ollie? In your face!

Anyway. I'm not dead, I'm really quite

clever.

And I'm starting again. So ignore the bit

you just read. Except this bit telling you to

ignore the other bit. Don't ignore that.

ignore

Monday

<u>Dear Diary</u>

That's how ladies in big dresses used to start their diaries in Days of Yore. They used to write diaries with feathers while they were waiting around for blokes to come round on horses with loads of money to marry them.

The blokes had loads of money, not the horses.

I don't want to get married. But if I did — only IF, mind — IF I did, I know who it would be!

It's someone with lovely brown eyes, but he doesn't even seem to see me. I'm not telling you any more yet, because first

I need to find a top-secret hiding place for my diary.

Dear Diary, would it be OK if I hid you in my pants drawer? They're all clean! I don't want Ollie to see you (smelly big brother).

Where did big-dress ladies of Yore hide their diaries? Did they have pants drawers?

Today my mum gave me this diary. I'd better tell you about my family. Also I'd better tell you about me. I'm going to do some underlining because I think it makes your work look neat.

Also I might underline important bits. I might do some highlighting as well I've got a yellow one that still works if you lick it.

Me

I'm Phoebe Dorcas Tonks. (My middle name is TOP SECRET - even to my friends) What were my parents thinking? Why didn't they call me Dork and be done with it?

I'm eleven and I've just gone to a big school made almost completely of glass. It has a soppy poem on the front about trying your best. You know the one!

It's huge (the school, not the poem) and it all looks the same. At the moment I keep getting lost. Why don't they paint different bits of the school different colours?

My teacher is very nice but she keeps forgetting my name. She had seven weeks off and she couldn't learn our names! She could have taken the list on the plane with her when she went on holiday, or she could have kept it for those long, boring moments in the toilet.

But no! She couldn't be bothered! Teachers get paid way too much!

'Phoebe' is pronounced 'fee' like the fee Mum had to pay when she parked at the back of the bank and they put clamps on the car, and 'bee' like the bee that stung her on the bottom while we were waiting for the very rude man to come and take the clamps off.

I learned some new words that afternoon!

Everyone just calls me 'Feely' because Oliver couldn't say 'Phoebe' when he was

little and just said
'Feely' in his cute little
baby voice. So, because
he had talking
problems, I got
lumbered with Feely
for the rest of my
days.

Not only that, Dad turned it into a joke:

'We call her 'Feely' because she is so
touchy! Ho! Ho! Ho!'

Every time someone asks, I hear the
same joke and I never get tired of it.
Always funny! I love to hear it again and
again. Not.

Mum (Susan Tonks)

Mum is a counsellor. She sorts out other people's problems. She mainly does sad and angry people.

Sometimes they are sad and angry at the same time. Sometimes they are just sad or just angry.

She's not so good at our problems though. When Ollie broke up with his girlfriend, she told him to 'Get over it, you're only fifteen'. I suppose she did change him from sad to angry. Does that count?

Mum works in a clinic down the road, so the sad and/or angry people don't come to our house, punching holes in our walls and dripping tears on our carpet.

Dad (Mark Tonks)

Dad is a teacher, which is funny because his name is Mark. Mark! Get it? Now that's funny!

If you have a problem like, for example, with girls calling you names, he always says,

'Just ignore them, they'll get tired of it'. Every time! He says it every time!'

Then he says:

'Sticks and stones will break my bones but names will never hurt me!' in a silly sing-song voice. And he looks like he's said something really clever.

He says his mum used to say that to him. That's sounds like rubbish, but it's not. It's a pile of mega-stinking-steaming rubbish! Grown-ups are crazy. No wonder people called him names.

The Parents

Together, Mum and Dad are: The Parents.

They might each be slightly rubbish on their

own, but together they are totally useless.

Mum is supposed to know lots about

people, but she knows nothing (nada – I'm

starting Spanish this year) about school.

Dad knows loads about school (targets

and rules and stuff) but he knows nada

about people.

Together, they don't help with problems – they just make everything worse. Together, they manage to get the worst out of every job.

Dad can cook and Mum can drive, but Mum does the cooking (she can burn fish fingers and Oliver once used one of her pancakes as a frisbee).

Dad does the driving. A tree drove into him last week.

They are like the black hole of problem solving.

Ollie

Oliver Wendell Tonks is my brother. He is also useless.

The thing about baby boys is that they are cute. He's my big brother, but I've seen the photos. He was a sweet baby.

He rolled about on a rug without his clothes on.

Then he grew and grew and now he's growing so fast he's a human bamboo – you can see him getting taller.

It's like kittens – they are cute and furry for like ten minutes, and then they grow up into big sleepy smelly cats and stink the place up.

We have no more room in our house for Ollie. He eats half a loaf as a snack and Mum yells at him at least ten times a day: 'Get out of that fridge, Oliver Tonks!'

Just like a cat, he sleeps a lot. He stays

in bed until midday on Saturdays and Mum

just leaves him (at least he's quiet and out

of the way).

Then he gets up and lies on the sofa.

The only times he's upright at the

weekends are when he goes out to play

football, or goes skateboarding, or hangs

around at the shopping centre looking at

girls.

Apart from that, he's always spread out somewhere and we have to step over him.

And the smells! Sweat, Lynx, trainers, Lynx, body odour, Lynx, feet, Lynx. And Lynx, Lynx, Lynx. It makes your eyes water.

My Problem

So these people I live with are no use to me. And I have a Huge Problem.

I'll tell you about it tomorrow.

tomorrow

Tuesday

Hi Diary!

Have you been having fun in the pants drawer? No, I wouldn't find it fun either.

Well this is my problem. There are some girls at school who are a gang. Mum says they are a clique. I thought she said 'click'

though, and because all their stuff is pink
and sparkly, in my head I call them the
Pink Click. They even have pink pens with
pink ink and pink
feathers on the top!

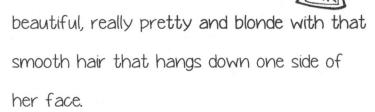

There are three of
them in the Click.

   Saffron is
beautiful, really pretty and blonde with that
smooth hair that hangs down one side of
her face.

   I think her family must be quite posh,
because she never stops talking about her
horse and her skiing holidays. I try not to,

really I do, but I just hate her.

She says these really
hurtful things and then she
gives a silly little giggle, as if
that makes it all OK.

Honestly, she is just evil.
She's the leader

Stacey has a face that's all pointy and

sharp. I bet you could spear
sausages with her nose. I bet
she has to sleep on her back
in case she stabs the pillow
with it! She's just as bad as
Saffron.

Then Daffy is sort of
short and chubby and
you'd think she was all
kind. Her hair stands out
round her head like a
dandelion seed. She looks
really sweet and cute.

Sometimes I think she's the worst of
the lot.

When the Pink Click are about, I try to
be invisible like one of those lizards that
turns the same colour as the thing it's on.
I try to go see-through and look like a shelf
of books or something.

It never works.

This week they 'noticed' me when we were in English. I said I'd read Harry Potter and I thought it was amazing.

The English teacher liked it too and we had a good chat about spells and Hogwarts and the Sorting Hat and stuff.

The Pink Click all turned and looked at me. It was like in the film when the pointy-faced mean dinosaurs notice a poor little park worker who is not a famous

actor. Their necks all turned round at the

same time and their

eyes went thin.

Perhaps the Pink

Click can't read at all?

Muggles!

What they did was shout after me:

'Feely, Feely you've dropped something!'

Then, when I turned around, they fell

about laughing. Everyone else laughed with

them. I felt awful. I tried not to cry.

Yesterday I got a tissue out just to dab

my face (OK, I was crying a bit) and

Saffron shouted:

'Feely, Feely don't drop your snotty tissue. We might skid on the snot!'

It's getting so I don't want to go to school. I feel sick in the mornings and I need the loo.

Mum could tell I was upset and I asked her what I should do. She said I should write a diary because 'it would help me get it all out' and 'I could think about it more clearly.'

I thought, 'What a giant load of old codswallop!'

But when I saw you, Diary, I fell in love with you.

I thought you would be a girly diary, all pink and sparkly with glitter that fell off and got on your face, and with tiny little pages with lines.

But no! You were a proper brown grown-up diary with heavy white paper, like something out of Harry Potter. (Mind you,

it's hard to write without lines – everything
goes up and down)

In this diary I'm going to write how I feel
now, so that I can remember it all when I'm
grown up. I will make shed-loads and
shed-loads of money and live in the huge
house at the end of our road.

I'm going to start my own school where
there will be no name-calling and you will be
able to go to Drama Club without people
making fun of you.

You are like a magic diary – please, please, *please* do some magic for me. Make Saffron walk through a magic door and disappear for ever!

If you don't help me, I don't know what I will do!

Wednesday

This morning I told Miss Rosy, my teacher, about the Huge Problem. She has an office like a big glass tank, so I had to do it quickly to stop the Pink Click seeing

If they saw me in there, they would know I was telling on them and they would get me for it.

'Fiona, honey,' she said, 'it is so good that you are telling me about this.'

'Phoebe.'

'We must treat this as a learning opportunity. We could have a little lesson on how to get on with people. All the class together, so nobody feels left out. Would you like that, um ... ?'

'Phoebe. No. Can't you just stop them doing it?'

'Well, Fay, it is better to encourage your

friends to be good, than to punish them for being bad, don't you think?'

It's Phoebe.'

No I didn't think.
Miss Rosy was
wrong. I wanted
them punished.
Horribly punished!
I wanted them
kept in after school.
I wanted them told
off by Mrs Harding,
the Head. What another huge fat load of

steaming codswallop!

Grown-ups are hopeless!

Oliver and his friend Danny (who is really nice and has gorgeous brown eyes and doesn't smell) were playing some noisy Xbox game when I got home.

I lugged my backpack with its four tons of homework through to the kitchen. I never take it upstairs — I'd never get it up there. The cello's bad enough.

In the sitting room Oliver had my diary. I must have left it on the coffee table.

What was I thinking? My heart when boom
– I was sure they must have read it and
had a good laugh.

But Oliver said they didn't even open it.

He said he would never read a person's
secret stuff. He said hand on his heart he
hadn't even thought of it.

I wouldn't believe Ollie because he is a
lying liar, but Danny backed him up and

smiled at me. Danny
wouldn't lie, I just
know it.

Anyway, dear Diary,
your magic isn't
working yet. Today Saffron called out in
the classroom:

'Feely, Feely what have you dropped –
oh it's only your aitches!'

Then Daffy shouted out:

'I thought you were going to say she'd
dropped her pants!'

The whole class laughed and
I felt my face go hot and red.

I think it's worse than rude to mention a person's pants in front of other people.

Tomorrow Saffron is doing a reading in assembly. She always gets picked for everything. Her hand is up before the teacher has stopped talking.

She has to walk up on stage. I hope she falls over! I hope her pants fall down!

Thursday

You did it! You did it, Diary! But it was a totally weird thing. I don't know how you did it, but I guess that's magic.

Just as Saffron was going to walk up the hall to the stage, Oliver's friend, Danny, clapped her on the back and said,

'Good luck, Saffron!'

He is like

totally fit, so she did her silly little giggle and went a bit pink. Well, pinker than usual.

Then, as she started walking, everyone
– I mean, everyone – could see she had a
sticky notice on her back. It said:

'MEAN GIRL'.

The whole school went quiet, but
Saffron must have thought they were
stunned by her amazing beauty or
something, because she kept walking.

Then, when a teacher told her – she was all the way to the front – she did a little scream and was in floods of tears and couldn't do the assembly.

Mrs Proud had to go on about litter and staying out of the toilets for twenty minutes, instead.

I've got to go now and phone all the members of Drama Club and talk about it.

Thank you Diary!

Friday

It just gets better and better. Saffron was very quiet at school today. Her mum came up to talk to our teacher, Miss Rosy, in her glass tank. At least, we could see Saffron's mum talking and Miss Rosy opening and shutting her mouth like a goldfish.

Saffron's mum is a School Governor, which is some sort of a big deal.

I asked Oliver why Danny had done it,

because he must have got into loads of trouble. I thought, maybe, Danny liked me a little bit.

Oliver said Danny just hates Saffron. He was going to put 'Big Bottom' on the notice, but he couldn't fit it in.

Then he wrote 'Big Bum', but he thought that some people with big bums are lovely. Saffron hasn't got a big bum anyway, it's tiny. It's a wonder she doesn't fall through those stools with holes in them in science.

So he decided on 'Mean Girl'. Danny had

been suspended for a day, which just

means working outside Mrs Harding's office,

where it is a bit smelly from the teachers'

toilets. He's not bothered.

Oliver said Danny couldn't know I was

having trouble with Saffron because they

hadn't read my diary – not that he knew

it was in there, because he didn't. As he

hadn't read it. At all. Not ever.

Then he pulled my hair and said:

'Stay cool, little sis!' which was nice because he usually tells me to drop dead.

Finally – just to make it perfect –
Saffron called after me again in class:

'Feely, Feely have you dropped something?'

and I said, quick as anything:

'Is it the notice that was on my back?
Oh no, I didn't have one!'

Everyone fell about, even Daffy and Stacey. I got into trouble with Miss Rosy ('That wasn't very nice, Fenella, was it?') but I didn't care.

I've got you to protect me, O Magic Diary!

About the author

Barbara Catchpole was a teacher for thirty years and enjoyed every minute. She has three sons of her own who were always perfectly behaved and never gave her a second of worry.

Barbara also tells lies.

How many have you read?

How many have you read?

Have you met  PIG?

Meet P.I.G - Peter Ian Green, although everybody calls him PIG for short. PIG lives with his mum.

He is small for his age, but says his mum is huge for hers. She is a single mum, but PIG says she looks more like a double mum or even a treble mum.

PIG and the Ice-cream Cake
Barbara Catchpole

PIG Skives off School
Barbara Catchpole

PIG is a Blue Baboon's Bottom
Barbara Catchpole

PIG SuperPig!
Barbara Catchpole

PIG and the Baldy Cat
Barbara Catchpole

PIG Leaves Home (for a bit)
Barbara Catchpole

PIG Whopping Great Fib

PIG is Hairy Snotter
Barbara Catchpole

PIG and the Rainbow Hair
Barbara Catchpole

PIG and the Big Quiz
Barbara Catchpole

PIG Gets Angry
Barbara Catchpole

PIG's Season's Finale
Barbara Catchpole